MW00762404

BEEKEEPERS

For Kala
(with thanks to Bob Hughes and Rainbow Apiaries)
—L.O.H.

To Skylar
—D.C.

BEEKEEPERS

by Linda Oatman High
Illustrated by Doug Chayka

Boyds Mills Press

WILLOUGHBY-EASTLAKE
PUBLIC LIBRARY

The springtime sunshine
pours like warm honey from the sky,
as Grandpa and I stand on the back porch,
before our morning chores.

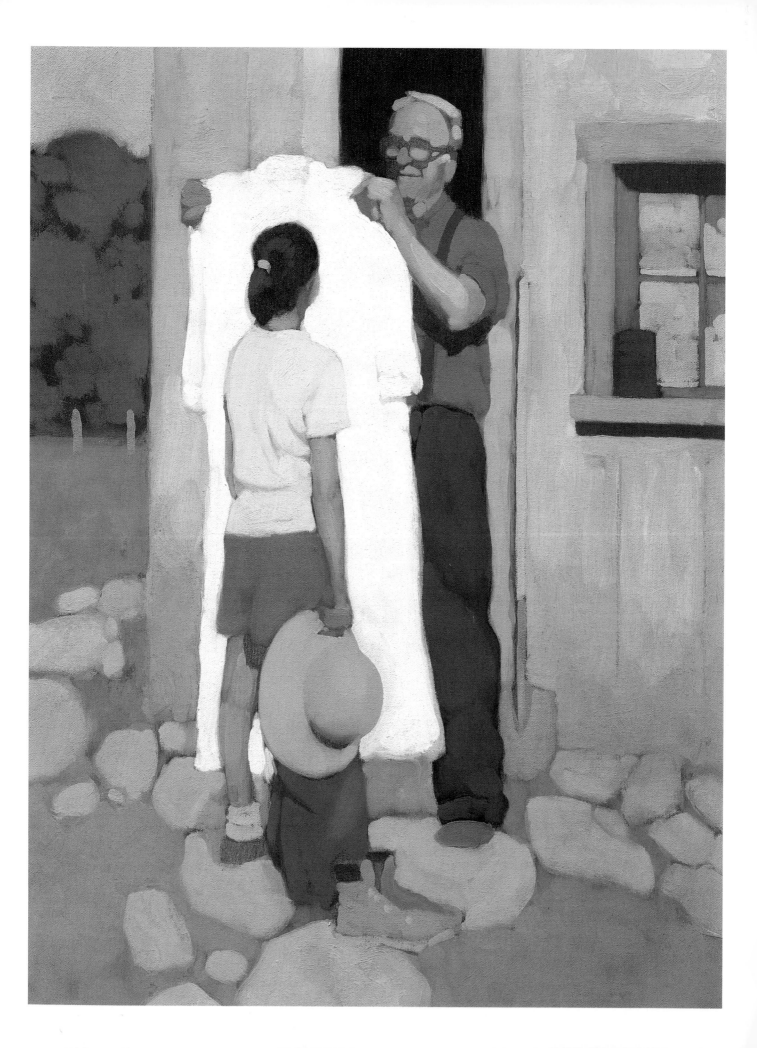

We dress:
long-sleeved white coveralls,
boots,
gloves,
and straw hats with
veils of mesh.

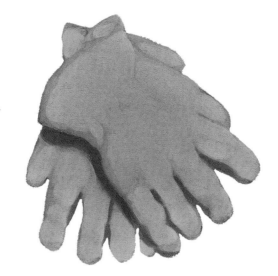

We walk across the grass,

dew misting our boots,

past the barn,

the pond,

the trees . . .

and into the bee yard.

The wooden hives are stacked high—
fronts facing the sun,

backs to the barn—
with a brick on each hive.

"Good morning, honeybees,"
Grandpa calls into the quietness,
his eyes sparkling behind the net.

I look up and see pods of pollen—
purple and pink,
yellow and orange,
blue and red and green—
gathered from springtime flowers and trees,
clinging to some of the bees.
"Every color of the rainbow," says Grandpa.
"The pollen gatherers have been working hard.
And now it's our turn."

I lift off bricks

and pry off the top covers with my hive tool

as Grandpa gives the bees a puff of smoke

from his bee smoker,

to quiet them and keep them from flying.

"Remember September?" Grandpa asks.

"All the bricks standing on end?"

"And July," I chime.

He nods and I smile,

thinking of honey

harvest times.

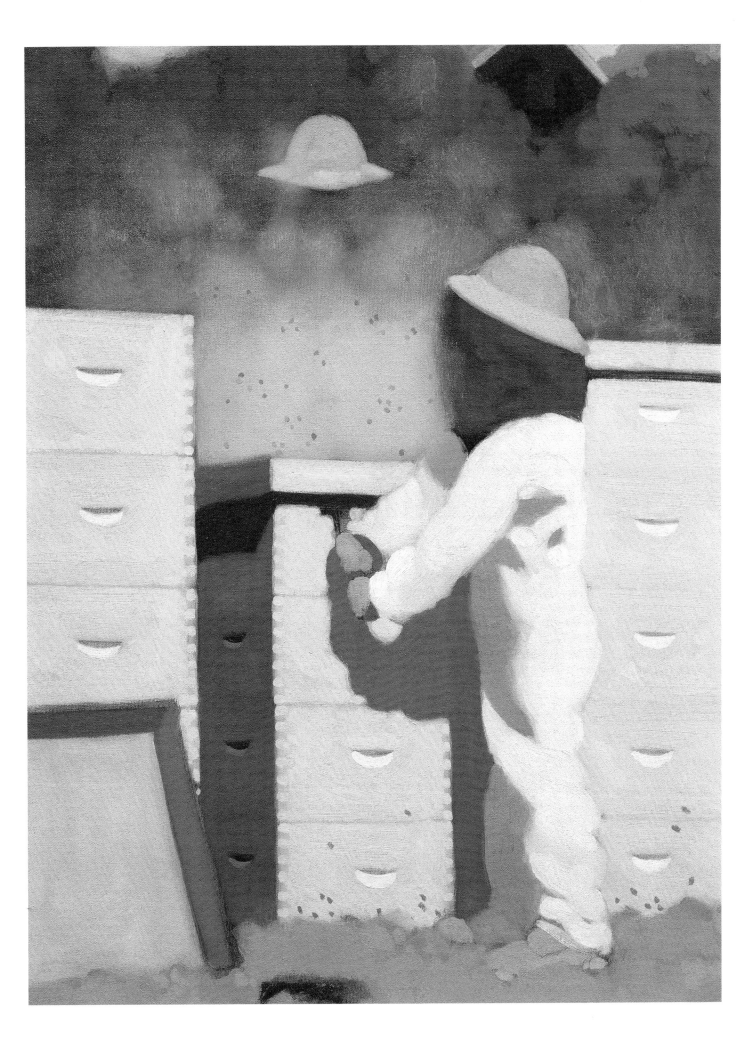

I close my eyes,

seeing the clear honey in the combs,

capped with snow-white wax.

I take a deep breath

remembering the sweet smell

of spun honey.

"Best open your eyes," Grandpa whispers.

"There's a swarm starting."

My eyes fly open and I catch my breath,
scared.

The sky darkens and buzzing fills my ears,
making my head spin.
Grandpa chuckles, softly,
eyes to the sky.
"Beautiful," he whispers.
The hum of the bees' wings grows
louder and louder,
and my heart races with the sound.

Standing still,
I hardly dare to breathe
as the bees twirl down like a tornado,
swirling and whirling every which way
above Grandpa and me,
then clustering on the branch of a tree.
Goosebumps sting my arms
and I shake,
wishing the swarm would settle.

Grinning,

Grandpa grabs his swarm-gathering tool:

a long pole with a hook on the end,

and an empty hive to place beneath the swarm.

He hands me the pole.

"Dislodge the swarm," he says.

My heart flies into my throat.

Bringing down the bees has always been Grandpa's job.

"What if they don't come?" I ask,

trembling.

Grandpa smiles.

"They'll come," he says.

I take a deep breath,

then hoist the pole into the cloud of bees.

Slowly,

I pull down the branch, shake it,

and a mass of bees plops down.

The swarm swirls around,

and soon,

thousands of bees are facing the hives,

heads bowed down and tails held high.

I sneak a glance at Grandpa and grin,

as the bees zoom into the hives.

Grandpa reaches over and takes the pole,

propping it against the fence.

"Their new home," he says,

as we watch the bees.

"They're settled, so the queen must be safe and

sound in the hive."

We leave the bee yard,
walking past the trees,
the pond,
the barn.
"A swarm in May is worth a load of hay," says
Grandpa as we walk.
"A swarm in June is worth a silver spoon," I say.
"A swarm in July isn't worth a fly," we say together,
laughing.

Grandpa lifts off his bee veil.

"Why do bees swarm?" I ask,

taking off my veil and gloves.

Grandpa shrugs.

"Why do spiders spin?" he asks.

We look at each other and smile.

"You're a fine keeper of bees," Grandpa says.

"First honey chunk of the season is all yours."

I nod,

proud,

as we walk up the porch steps and into the house,

springtime sunshine like warm honey

across our backs.

Text copyright © 1998 by Linda Oatman High
Illustrations © 1998 by Doug Chayka
All rights reserved

Published by Caroline House
Boyds Mills Press, Inc.
A Highlights Company
815 Church Street
Honesdale, Pennsylvania 18431
Printed in Hong Kong

Publisher Cataloging-in-Publication Data
High, Linda Oatman.
    Beekeepers / by Linda Oatman High ; illustrated by
Doug Chayka.—1st ed.
[32]p. : col.ill. ; cm.
Summary : A young girl helps her grandfather tend his bee
hives one morning in Spring.
ISBN 1-56397-486-X
1. Grandfathers—Fiction—Juvenile literature. 2. Beekeepers—
Juvenile literature—Fiction. [1. Grandfathers—Fiction. 2.
Beekeepers—Fiction.]
I. Chayka, Doug, ill. II. Title.
    [E]—dc20   1998   AC   CIP
Library of Congress Catalog Card Number 97-72047

First edition, 1998
Book designed by Tim Gillner
The text of this book is set in 18-point Palatino.
The illustrations are done in oil.

10 9 8 7 6 5 4 3 2 1

J - 3-4

MAR 2 4 1998

J - 3-4